George Brown, CLASS CLOWN

Attack of the Tighty Whities!

visit us at www.abdopublishing.com

Reinforced library bound edition published in 2014 by Spotlight, a division of the ABDO Group, PO Box 398166, Minneapolis, MN 55439. Spotlight produces high-quality reinforced library bound editions for schools and libraries. Published by agreement with Grosset & Dunlap, a division of Penguin Young Readers Group.

Printed in the United States of America, North Mankato, Minnesota.
102013
012014

 This book contains at least 10% recycled materials.

Library of Congress Cataloging-in-Publication Data

This title was previously cataloged with the following information:

Krulik, Nancy E.
   Attack of the tighty whities! / by Nancy Krulik ; illustrated by Aaron Blecha.
   p. cm. -- (George Brown, Class Clown)
   Summary: George is representing his school at the county-wide spelling bee, and hopes to compete without getting overpowered by an embarrassing, magic super burp.
   [1. Behavior--Fiction. 2. Belching--Fiction. 3. Spelling bees--Fiction. 4. Schools--Fiction. 5. Magic--Fiction.] I. Title. II Series.
   PZ7.K9416 At 2012
   E--dc23   2011018036

ISBN 978-1-61479-215-4 (Reinforced Library Bound Edition)

All Spotlight books are reinforced library binding
and manufactured in the United States of America.

For Danny B.—NK

For Grandma LaVerne—AB

George Brown, CLASS CLOWN

Attack of the Tighty Whities!

by Nancy Krulik
illustrated by Aaron Blecha

Grosset & Dunlap
An Imprint of Penguin Group (USA) Inc.

Chapter 1

"Okay, Louie," Mrs. Kelly said. "Spell *crabby*."

It was the last round of Edith B. Sugarman Elementary School's fourth-grade spelling bee. There were only two spellers left: Louie Farley and George Brown. They were standing on the stage of the school auditorium.

George frowned as Louie got ready to spell. *Crabby* was **an easy word**. Louie was bound to get it right.

Louie sure *looked* confident. He smiled and nodded. "Crabby," he repeated. "C-r-a-b-y. Crabby."

Louie got the word wrong! All George had to do was spell it right, and he would be the winner.

"I'm sorry, Louie," Mrs. Kelly said. "That is incorrect. George, can *you* spell *crabby?*"

George walked to the mic. "Crabby," he said. "C-r-a-b-b-y. Crabby."

"Th-that's what I meant," Louie stammered. "Two *b*'s." He looked over to his friends, Mike and Max, for help. **But they didn't know what to say.**

Mrs. Kelly gave George one of her big, gummy grins. It looked like Mrs. Kelly had eaten oatmeal for breakfast. *Yuck.*

"Congratulations, George," Mrs. Kelly said. "You're **the winner**! That means you will be the fourth-grade contestant at **next week's county-wide spelling bee**."

"Wahoo!" George's best friend Alex shouted. "George is the champ!"

"Go, champ! Go, champ!" George's other good friend Chris cheered.

Soon all the kids were cheering. Well, all the kids except Louie's pals, Mike and Max.

Louie looked like someone had **punched him in the gut**—or like he wanted to punch *someone else* in the gut. Either way, he seemed upset.

"But that's not fair," Louie insisted. "I meant to put that other *b* in there. I just forgot."

"I'm sorry, Louie," Mrs. Kelly said. "But there's always next year."

George walked offstage and joined his classmates.

"Congratulations, dude," Alex said. "That was **awesome**."

"I didn't even get past the first round," Chris added. "Who knew *flight* wasn't spelled with an *e* on the end?"

George knew that. He knew a lot about spelling.

"You have to train hard from now on," Julianna told George. "The words in the county-wide spelling bee are going to be **really tough**."

George gulped.

"Don't worry," Julianna assured him. "We'll all help."

"Thanks," George said.

Sage gave George **a goofy smile** and blinked her eyelashes up and down. "Oh,

Georgie," she said. "You were amazing. It was like you had a dictionary in your head."

George frowned. He hated when Sage called him *Georgie*. Still, it was cool having all his friends act like he was **some sort of genius**.

"You were robbed," George could hear Max telling Louie as they all returned to their classroom. "You knew how to spell *crabby*. **You're an expert on crabby.**"

"Yeah," Mike agreed. "You're like the crabbiest person I know."

Louie shot Mike a look.

"I mean in a good way," Mike added quickly.

Louie shrugged. "George just got lucky. He'll **never win** the county-wide. Two years ago, my brother, Sam, came in third place. And he is way smarter than George."

"Maybe George will come in second place," Chris told Louie.

9

"Or even first," Sage added. "George is smart enough to come in first."

"No way," Louie insisted. "And besides, he'll probably do something goofy and **mess up**."

George frowned. He knew what Louie meant. George was always doing goofy things that got him into trouble. But it wasn't his fault. **It was all because of that rotten super burp!**

It all started when George and his family first moved to Beaver Brook. George's dad was in the army, so the family moved around a lot. George had lots of experience being the new kid in school. He'd expected the first day in his new school to stink. First days always did.

But *this* first day was the stinkiest.

In his old school, George had been the class clown. He was always pulling **pranks** and making jokes. But George

had promised himself that things were going to be **different** at Edith B. Sugarman Elementary School. He was turning over a new leaf. No more pranks. No more whoopee cushions or paper airplanes. He wasn't going to get into any trouble anymore. He wasn't going to make funny faces or goof on his teachers behind their backs.

George didn't have to be a math whiz like Alex to figure out how many friends you make being the unfunny, well-behaved new kid in school. The answer was easy. **Zero. Nada. Zilch.** And that's exactly how many friends George had made by the end of his first day at Edith B. Sugarman Elementary School. **None.**

That night, George's parents took him out to Ernie's Ice Cream Emporium. While they were sitting outside and George was finishing his root beer float, **a shooting star flashed across the sky**. So George made a wish.

I want to make kids laugh—but not get into trouble.

Unfortunately, the star was gone before George could finish the wish. **So only half came true**—the first half.

A minute later, **George had a**

funny feeling in his belly. It was like there were hundreds of tiny bubbles bouncing around in there. The bubbles hopped up and down and all around. They **ping-ponged** their way into his chest and **bing-bonged** their way up into his throat. And then . . .

George let out a big burp. A *huge* burp. A SUPER burp!

The super burp was loud, and it was *magic.*

Suddenly George lost control of his arms and legs. It was like they had minds of their own. His hands grabbed straws and stuck them up his nose like a walrus. His feet jumped up on the table

and started dancing the **hokey-pokey**. Everyone at Ernie's Ice Cream Emporium started laughing— except George's parents, who were covered in ice cream from the sundaes he had knocked over.

The magical super burps came back lots of times after that. And every time a burp arrived, it brought trouble with it. Like the time it made him **act like a dog** and start barking during the fourth-grade field day.

He'd even licked Principal McKeon's hand! *Blech!*

And then there was the time the

burp **exploded** during Louie's water park birthday party. George went crazy on a tubing ride. He dived underwater and started pinching people's butts! Boy, were the lifeguards mad at him! Louie's mom was plenty angry, too.

But Mrs. Farley wasn't nearly as mad as George's mom had been the time the magical super burp showed up at her craft store, the Knit Wit. George wound up wrapping himself in cloth and crashing his way through the rows of craft supplies like a **crazed, polka-dotted mummy**. By the time the burp disappeared, the store was a mess.

The super burp had gotten George into lots and lots of trouble. **None of it had been his fault.** But George couldn't tell anyone that. They wouldn't believe him even if he did. George wouldn't have believed it, either—if he weren't the one it was happening to.

The only person who knew about the magical super burp was Alex. George was really lucky that his best friend could keep a secret—and that he was willing to try and help George find a way to **squelch that belch** once and for all.

Unfortunately, Alex hadn't come up with a solution yet. George sure hoped he would find one soon. **The county-wide spelling bee was less than a week away.** A burp at the bee would be a disaster— **D-I-S-A-S-T-E-R!**

Chapter 2

"Dude, you hungry?" Alex asked George when the boys arrived at Alex's house after school.

"Oh yeah!" George knew that Alex's kitchen was always stocked with great stuff—stacks of peanut butter crackers, cartons of cookies, and gallons of ice cream.

"How about a **vanilla ice-cream and onion shake**?" Alex asked him.

George made a face. That was not the kind of snack he had in mind. "Vanilla ice cream and *onion*?"

Alex nodded. "Yeah. I read on this website that eating onions can help people stop **feeling gassy** all the time. And milk or cream will line your stomach so you don't . . . well . . . you know . . ."

George *did* know. "So I don't burp," he said, finishing Alex's sentence.

"Exactly."

"Isn't there some other way?" George asked. He didn't want to seem ungrateful, but onions and ice cream sounded **disgusting**.

Alex shrugged. "Not that I know of." He reached into a drawer in the refrigerator and pulled out a big onion. "Besides, how bad can it taste?"

Alex got out a blender, and soon it was making whirring sounds, mixing up milk, ice cream, and onions.

Awful. That's how bad that shake

tasted when George took a sip. Holding his nose didn't help. It was really, really disgusting. George didn't think anything

could make vanilla ice cream taste rotten. **But an onion did the trick.**

"Aren't *you* going to drink any?" George asked Alex. The blender was still half full.

Alex shook his head. "That's all for you, buddy. I'm having a banana and peanut butter sandwich. You better drink up if you want to get rid of those giant burps."

The super burps were definitely **king-size**. So George pinched his nose again. "Here goes," he said as he took another huge gulp and tried not to gag.

"You think it's working? Any burplike symptoms?" Alex asked George an hour later while the boys were busy playing video games in Alex's living room.

"Nope. So far, so good," George said. He clicked a button and destroyed a spaceship on the screen. "I'm a gas-free guy!"

"Um . . . dude?" Alex asked. "You mind looking the other way when you talk? **Your breath stinks.** It must be the onions."

George wrinkled his nose. His breath was so bad, even he could tell it stunk. And it was pretty hard to smell your own breath. Still, having bad breath was worth it—if it was burp-free breath.

"You got any gum?" George asked Alex.

"Just my already been chewed gum ball," Alex said.

Alex was going for the world's record for making the **biggest ABC gum ball**. One day he hoped to get in the *Schminess Book*

of World Records. George couldn't ask him to sacrifice a piece of ABC gum. Especially since George knew where some of that gum came from—sidewalks, under desks, and **behind toilet seats**.

"That's okay," George told Alex. "I'll just move over so you don't smell me as much."

"An *onion and vanilla ice-cream* shake?" George's mom asked him later that afternoon when she picked him up to drive him to the mall. "What made you want to drink something like that?"

Uh-oh. **How was George going to explain this one?** It wasn't like he could tell his mom about the super burps.

"It just sounded cool," George told her.

"I wish I had a mint or something," his mom said.

"Do we really have to go shopping?" George asked, changing the subject.

George's mom smiled. "Of course we do. The minute you told me about **the county-wide spelling bee**, shopping was all I could think of."

How **weird**. George hadn't thought about going shopping once.

"You have to dress for success. Look good and you will *be* good," his mom continued. "And there will probably be a photographer from the newspaper."

"I guess," George said.

George's mom made a face. "Honey, do you mind sticking your face out the window?" she asked. "Your breath is really stinking up the car."

George rolled down the window. The wind hit his face. He opened his mouth and stuck his tongue out, **just like a dog**. The wind blew into his mouth. But nothing burst back out. He'd been burp-free all afternoon. Maybe an onion shake a day *could* keep the burp away.

Chapter 3

"Let me see how you look," George's mother called to him.

George was inside a dressing room in the boys' section of Mabel's Department Store. He stared at himself in the mirror. He did *not* want to come out. His mother had made him try on **plaid pants and a white shirt with a bow tie**.

"Come on, George," his mother called again. "I don't have all day."

Squeak. Squeak. Squeak. The plaid pants made noises as he walked.

"Oh my!" George's mother shouted.

"My little man looks so handsome."

"Mom," George whispered. "Do you have to talk so loud?"

"Don't you think he looks handsome?" George's mom asked the salesman. "Did I mention that he's going to be in **a county-wide spelling bee**?"

"Yeah, I think you did," the salesman said. He didn't look **impressed**.

"Can you spell *plaid*?" George's mom asked him as she straightened his bow tie.

"P-l-a-i-d," George said.

"Exactly right," his mother said.

"I hate these pants," George said. **"They squeak."**

His mother frowned. "Okay, then try on the beige slacks."

"Can't I get the black jeans and the leather jacket instead?" George asked her hopefully.

His mom shook her head. "This is a spelling bee, not a skateboarding contest."

George went back into the dressing room. **The beige slacks were even worse than the plaid pants.**

"And don't forget the red suspenders," his mom called to him.

George groaned. But he did as he was told. Then he looked in the mirror. He looked like his mother's uncle Milton **who was eighty-three**.

"*Grrr,*" George grumbled under his

breath as he walked out of the dressing room.

Right away, George heard **a terrible sound**. Somebody was laughing. George knew that laugh anywhere. The laugh was mean. **It was Louie's laugh.**

"Nice suspenders," Louie said as he walked over to George. "I think my grandfather has a pair just like them."

George couldn't believe it. This was a nightmare. N-I-G-H-T-M-A-R-E.

"George, aren't you going to introduce me to your friend?" his mother asked.

None of George's friends were in the store. But he figured his mother meant Louie.

"This is Louie," George muttered under his breath.

"Man, your breath smells like vomit," Louie whispered.

"At least I can spell *vomit*," George whispered back. It wasn't a great comeback.

"Hi, Louie," George's mom said. "We're getting George some clothes for the county-wide spelling bee."

Just then, Louie's mom joined them. She was holding a hanger with a **black leather skateboarding jacket**.

"That's the jacket I'm getting," Louie said.

George frowned. **No fair!** Louie didn't even have a skateboard. He had sneakers with wheels that popped out. But that wasn't the same thing at all. He didn't need a black, leather jacket. Not like George did.

Louie's mom looked at George and frowned. She remembered him from Louie's birthday party. Considering all the things the burps had made him do, her memories probably weren't too great.

"We're closing in fifteen minutes," the salesman told George's mom. "Is there anything else your son wants to try on?"

George's mom shook her head. "I guess not. We'll take the slacks, the shirt, the suspenders, the bow tie, and . . . oh! **Two packages of underpants.**"

The salesman nodded and walked

off. A moment later he returned with the underwear.

George went into the dressing room and changed back into his own T-shirt and jeans. They felt so much better than the new pants and shirt. As he came out, he handed the new stuff to his mother.

"I have to run upstairs and return something in the lingerie department," she told him. "We can go and pay for everything there."

Uh-oh. George knew what *lingerie* meant. **Ladies' underwear.**

"Mom," George pleaded. "Don't make me go with you."

"I guess you could stay here with **your buddy Louie**," his mom suggested.

Louie's mom's eyes narrowed. She frowned at George again. "We're . . . um . . . we're just about done here, and we have to run," she told George's mom.

Then she grabbed Louie, and they left.

"Listen, Mom," George said. "I'll just sit right here on the bench next to the escalator. I won't move. I promise."

George's mom thought about that for a second. "Okay," she said finally. **"Spell escalator."**

"E-s-c-a-l-a-t-o-r," George spelled.

His mom smiled. "That's my boy!"

George felt really grown-up sitting by himself on the bench by the escalator.

He
liked
watching
the silver,
metal stairs go
up, up, up.
Then, suddenly,
George felt something
funny in his tummy. Bing . . .
bong. Ping . . . **pong**.
Uh-oh. The bubbles in George's belly were
trying to go up, up, up, and *out*.

BUUURP!

Chapter 4

The burp was so loud all the clothes on the racks started to shake. Everyone in the boys' department turned to stare. George opened his mouth to say, "Excuse me." But all that came out was **"Burp—that's spelled b-u-r-p."**

That was not a spelling bee word, but **the burp was in charge now**.

Just then, George's eyes spotted a boy mannequin wearing a pair of jeans and a Beaver Brook Beagles football jersey. George's legs raced toward it.

"TACKLE!" George's mouth shouted. He **pounced** on the mannequin.

"Young man!" a salesman shouted. "Stop that!"

The mannequin tipped over. Both its arms came off.

George held the arms in the air. "Someone call an ambulance!" George's mouth called out. "This guy's lost his arms! He needs a doctor! **STAT!**"

George had no idea what "stat" meant. But the burp must have known because it made his mouth say it.

George waved the mannequin's arms in the air. "Hi!" he shouted to customers until a salesman hurried over and grabbed the mannequin's arms from George.

"Oh, thank you, kind sir, for helping!" George shouted and **hugged the salesman**, who was having a hard time putting the arms back.

"Young man, where is your mother?" the salesman asked George. "Leave before you get in any more trouble."

Trouble was what the burp liked best!

George's eyes fell on a stack of hats across the aisle. He ran over and began piling them on his head, one on top of the other. **His head was happy because now it was getting into trouble, too.**

"Caps for sale," George's mouth shouted as he paraded around the floor with a stack of hats on his head. "Caps for sale."

A three-year-old boy in a stroller took his thumb out of his mouth and looked up at his mom. "I want that green hat," the little boy said.

"Sure! Have a green one!" George said. He **tossed the green cap** to the boy. Then he threw another hat at him.

"Have a red one, too!"

"I only want green," the little kid said.

George's arms reached up and began to throw the hats off his head, one at a time.

"Here's a blue hat." George threw a blue baseball cap in the air. "And a yellow one!" Suddenly, caps were flying everywhere!

Whee! A red hat flew over a display of socks.

Whish! A yellow baseball cap soared over a rack of little boys' overalls.

Whooeee! A black hat flew up high and landed on a light fixture.

By now, a circle of salespeople had surrounded George. One of them pulled out his cell phone. George had a feeling he was calling a guard.

George was cornered. His legs decided to make a break for it. Squirming through salesmen, George felt

41

himself **propelled** right toward the down escalator.

Whoa! All of a sudden George was **running *up* the down escalator**.

"Hey, kid. Watch where you're going," a passenger shouted.

George's legs climbed up the metal stairs faster and faster. A woman with lots of shopping bags tried to move out of the path of the oncoming George.

She was too late. George plowed into her.

The woman's packages went flying. A pair of shoes fell out and started going down the escalator without her. A sweater flew out of another bag. It landed on the shoulders of the man in front of her.

"This isn't mine," the man said.

"Will you **turn around** and go the right way?" the woman shouted at George. But George's feet kept **marching** up, up, up—as the escalator stairs went down, down, down.

Up. Up. Up.

Down. Down. Down.

Whoosh!

Just then, George felt something go **pop**. It was as if someone had just punctured a balloon in the bottom of his belly. **All the air rushed out of him.** The super burp was gone.

The salespeople were all still there, too, waiting for him. So was the woman with the spilled packages and the man with the women's sweater. They all looked ma-a-ad. George knew he had to **get out of there** quickly. If his mother found out what had happened, he'd be in trouble—T-R-O-U-B-L-E!

So George climbed up the down escalator as fast as he could. At last he reached the next floor. He spotted his mother at the cash register. She was paying for some white, lacy things. **George shut his eyes** so he wouldn't have to look at them.

"George," his mom said when she spotted

him. "You were supposed to wait for me downstairs."

"I . . . um . . . **I got bored**," George told her.

"All right," his mom said, taking her bag and handing George his to carry. "Time to head home." She started to walk toward the escalators.

Uh-oh. George gulped. That gang of salespeople was probably still waiting for him on the floor below.

"Forget the escalator," he told his mom quickly. "Let's take the elevator. **It's much faster.**"

Chapter 5

"So the onion milkshake didn't work?" Alex said the next morning when he and George met up on the school playground. "That's a **bummer**."

"Tell me about it," George agreed. He wiggled a little and pulled at his pants. The new tighty whities were **a little *too* tight**. "At least Louie was gone before the burp exploded."

Alex smiled at George. "Don't worry. I'll do more research. There's got to be a way to stop the . . ."

"Shhh," George interrupted him. "Julianna and Chris are coming over." He felt bad about keeping secrets from his pals, but the fewer people who knew about the burps, the better.

Alex zipped his lips, quick.

"Hey, guys," Julianna said.

"What's up?" Chris asked.

"George was just telling me how his mom made him go shopping for **spelling bee clothes**," Alex said.

"That's just what I wanted to talk to you about," Julianna told George.

Huh? That was **weird**. Sure, most girls liked to talk about shopping. But not Julianna. The only thing that interested her was sports.

"Well, we went to Mabel's Department Store," George told her. "I ended up getting a pair of pants and . . ."

Julianna cut him off. "I don't mean the

clothes. I want to talk to you about the spelling bee. I want to **tape an interview with you** about how you're training for it for my sports report."

Julianna was the fourth-grade sportscaster on the school's closed-circuit TV station, WEBS TV. So that made more sense. Sort of. But not exactly.

"What does a stupid spelling bee have to do with sports?" Louie asked. He, Mike, and Max had walked over to where George and his friends were standing.

"Excuse me, but she wasn't talking to you!" George said.

"Since you're asking, Louie, here's why," Julianna said. "**It's a competition.** And it takes training, like any other competition."

"Who wants to listen to George talk about spelling?" Louie asked.

"Not me," Max said.

"Me neither," Mike said. "Boring—b-o-r-r-i-n-g!"

"That's b-o-r-i-n-g," George corrected him. "There's only **one r**." Then he turned to Julianna. "Want me to try standing on my hands? Then I could spell **upside down**."

"Sure," said Julianna.

"Now, spell *banana*," Chris said.

"B-a-n-a-n—" George began to spell as he sprang straight up on his hands.

"What a dweeb," Louie said. He walked away in disgust with Mike and Max trailing after him.

George smiled—of course, since he was upside down, his smile looked like a frown. **But it was still a smile.** He loved making Louie mad.

A few minutes later, George and his pals were all seated at their desks. Mrs. Kelly had written the date on the board. March 31.

That meant tomorrow was April 1. April Fools' Day. When you pulled pranks on people and made them do stupid things. George gulped. **He had a funny feeling that April Fools' was the super burp's favorite holiday!** Things could get really out of control. *Even more than usual.*

"Good morning, class," Mrs. Kelly said. "Tomorrow is April 1. And at Edith B. Sugarman Elementary School, you know what that means."

George looked at his teacher curiously. He was the new kid. He had **no idea** what that meant.

But everyone else did. "Backward Day!" they all shouted.

"That's right," Mrs. Kelly said. "Which means everything that happens tomorrow is going to be backward. You should wear your clothing backward. We'll run our class schedule starting with last period. There will be breakfast for lunch and all sorts of other fun, backward events."

She beamed **a wide smile** at George. She'd had scrambled eggs this morning. "Maybe our spelling champ will even spell words backward for us."

George had always liked Backward Day at his old school. Last year, he and his buddy Kadeem told lots of jokes—only they each gave **the punch line first**, and the other kid had to figure out the riddle question.

But last year, George had only burped like a **normal kid**. Suddenly he had a terrible thought. What if the super burps decided to go backward? What if instead of bursting out of his mouth, they blasted out of his other end?

Chapter 6

"Dude, you have to help me," George told Alex as the boys left school at the end of the day. "Tomorrow, **what if the burp goes backward**? Think about it!"

"Ooh, that's a nasty thought," Alex said. Then he thought for a moment. "Look, George. The first thing you have to do is **chill out**," Alex warned him. "All my research shows that being stressed can give you gas."

George took a deep breath and tried to relax. But it wasn't easy.

"And stay away from beans tonight," Alex added. "'Cause you know what they do."

"Right. No beans," George agreed.

He took another **big breath**.

Just then, Chris came over to where the boys were standing. "What are you guys doing this afternoon?" he asked.

"George is stressed out about the . . . uh . . . spelling bee," Alex said. "I want him to stay chill."

"Julianna and I are going over to her uncle Harry's miniature golf course," Chris said. "It's opening day for the season. You want to come?"

Alex looked at George. "Whenever my dad gets all stressed, he goes out to hit a few golf balls."

"Okay," George said. Then he laughed. "But maybe I should run home and get another pair of pants, just in case."

Julianna looked at him. "In case of what?"

"In case I get a hole in one," George said.

His friends all laughed. George smiled.

He loved it when his friends liked his jokes. It was like how things used to be at his old school.

Too bad Backward Day couldn't take George back in time—to the days before the big burp bing-bonged its way into his life.

"I've been playing miniature golf here ever since I was little," Julianna said as she and the boys lined up at the first hole later that afternoon.

"Miniature . . . m-i-n-i-a-t-u-r-e," George spelled. He looked around. Each hole on the mini-golf course was based on **a famous fairy tale**.

"My favorite is the *Snow White* hole," Julianna said as she handed George a yellow golf ball. "The witch spins around like a windmill, so you have to time it just right to get your ball over to the hole without her blocking it. The *Aladdin* hole is cool, too, because if you manage to hit your ball onto the little, flying carpet, it takes off and lands you **a hole in one**."

George knew all about the *Aladdin* story. He also knew what he would wish for if he had **a magic genie**—he'd wish for the super burp to disappear!

"The *Alice in Wonderland* hole is fun," Julianna

continued as she handed Chris a white golf ball. "It's got a rabbit hole, a rose garden, and a mouse who pops up and down out of a teapot. And at the *Three Billy Goats Gruff* hole, you have to get your ball over the bridge before **a mechanical troll pops up and blocks it**."

"That seems really hard," Alex said.

"It is." Julianna put her blue ball at the start of the *Jack and the Beanstalk* hole.

"B-e-a-n-s-t-a-l-k," George spelled out.

Julianna frowned. "Are you going to spell at every hole?" she asked. "Because that's going to break my concentration."

"S-o-r-r-y," George spelled. Alex and Chris both laughed.

But Julianna didn't. Instead, she laid her golf club down on the green felt and **eyed it carefully**.

"What are you doing?" George asked her.

"Measuring out a straight line between here and the giant's hand," Julianna explained. "The ball slides down his arm and lands near the hole."

"She's really serious about this, isn't she?" Alex said to Chris.

"Julianna takes all sports seriously,"

George said. "Seriously. S-e-r . . ." He stopped when Julianna turned and gave him **a dirty look**.

"A Toiletman mini-golf course would be cool," Chris told the boys. Toiletman was a superhero Chris invented.

"You could make all the holes look like mini toilets," George told Chris. "The first hole could be called **the Royal Flush**. And then maybe you could have brown golf balls and . . ."

"Gross! Will you guys stop it?" Julianna asked. "I'm trying to concentrate here!"

George frowned. Playing mini golf with Julianna wasn't exactly relaxing.

Chapter 7

Finally, Julianna hit the ball. "All right!" she shouted as it landed in the palm of the giant's hand and flew into the little cup at the edge of the green. **"A hole in one."** She smiled. "Who wants to go next?"

George managed to get the ball in the cup in three hits. Chris and Alex each took four. Then they all moved on to the *Alice in Wonderland* hole.

"The goal here is to get your ball to go down the rabbit hole," Julianna said, pointing. "And stay away from the rose garden, because it's almost impossible to get out of there."

The rose garden looked like a maze. George could see that would be a problem.

But that wasn't the only problem George had. All of a sudden, he felt some wild bubbling in his belly. **Ping-pong. Bing-bong!**

Oh no! The super burp was back! George shut his mouth tight and tried to keep the burp from slipping out.

But the super burp wasn't about to let two little lips keep it from **bursting out**. Already it was **bing-bonging** its way around George's kidneys and **ping-ponging** over his liver.

George tried remembering the signal he and Alex had about the burp. If George gave the signal, Alex would grab him and get him somewhere he couldn't cause any trouble.

Was he supposed to rub his belly and pat his head? Or pat his belly and rub his head? Or . . .

B-U-U-U-R-P!

Too late.

George let out a major burp. It was so loud that Julianna's golf ball actually **popped back out of the hole**.

"Uh-oh . . . ," Alex said. "George. Don't . . ."

George's legs immediately went into action. They ran over to the *Three Billy Goats Gruff* hole and began dancing across the bridge. **George got down on all fours.** "*Maaaa . . . maaaa . . .*," his mouth bleated as he crawled over the bridge.

"Hey, that's pretty good," Chris laughed.

"You really sound like a billy goat."

"Get off of there," Julianna insisted. "My uncle's going to get mad."

Boy, was Julianna right. Just then, her uncle Harry came rushing over. "Julianna!" he shouted. "Get your friend off of there!"

Whoosh! Suddenly, George felt something go pop. **It was like a balloon burst in his belly.** All the air rushed out of him.

The super burp was gone. But George was still there on the *Three Billy Goats*

Gruff bridge. "Get over here right now!" Julianna's uncle demanded.

George did as he was told. He slid off the bridge. Then he opened his mouth to say, "I'm sorry." And that's exactly what came out.

"I can't believe you got us thrown out," Julianna grumbled a few minutes later as she and the boys walked home. "I bet my uncle tells my mother."

George frowned. He didn't want to get Julianna in trouble. **Louie's mom already hated him.** If things kept going this way, every mom in Beaver Brook was going to have it in for him.

Stupid super burp. It was worse than any witch, troll, or giant could ever be. **It was *real*.**

Chapter 8

Alex started laughing as soon as George walked onto the playground the next morning.

George grinned. He was wearing his **new underwear over his pants** so everyone could see them. It was Backward Day after all. "I like your **backward sweatshirt**," George told Alex.

"My mom had to zip it for me," Alex said. "It's hard to zip when the zipper's in the back." He stopped for a minute and looked at George. "How's your stomach feeling?"

"Okay for now," George said. "I didn't eat any beans last night. And I didn't have root beer, either. Root beer can cause real stomach trouble." He stopped and smiled. "Did you know *stomach* is spelled with a silent *h* at the end? It was one of the words on last night's spelling list. My mom is coaching me."

Just then, Louie came rolling over on his sneakers with wheels. He was wearing his new leather jacket backward. Max and Mike were walking behind Louie. They were both wearing their baseball caps backward.

"I see England, I see France, I see George's underpants," Louie sang out.

George rolled his eyes. "Duh. You're *supposed* to see my underpants. I'm wearing my clothes in backward order. It's about as backward as it gets."

"No way," Max said. "Louie's more

backward than you."

"Yeah," Mike added. "Everybody's always talking about how backward Louie is."

"Do something backward, Louie," Mike urged.

Louie grinned. "Like this?" he asked as he started **skating backward** on his wheelie sneakers all around the yard.

Bam! Louie's wheels slid out from under him.

"Ouch!"

Louie landed on his rear.

George and Alex laughed. Mike and Max laughed a little, too—until Louie **glared** at them.

"What are you laughing at?" Louie asked George. He sounded really, really mad.

George stopped laughing. It was safer that way. Because from the look on Louie's face, it seemed like he was ready to knock George *backward* to last Tuesday. And if anyone could do that, it was Louie!

A few minutes later, George saw Mrs. Kelly waiting for everybody at the door to their classroom. She was wearing **a red, flannel bathrobe and bunny slippers**. And she had **curlers** in her hair. "I'm ready for bed, which is what I do at the *end* of the day," she explained.

"That sure is very backward of you,
Mrs. Kelly," George said.

Suddenly, out of nowhere, George's teacher began dancing. *"Hello, I must be going,"* she sang. *"I came to say, I cannot stay, I must be going."*

Mrs. Kelly was definitely **one weird teacher**. But she was nice, too. It took a lot of guts to dance around the classroom in a nightgown and **bunny slippers**.

Mrs. Kelly finished her song and dance and walked up to the front of the room. "Okay, class, take your seats," she said. "It's time to get started."

George raised his hand. "Don't you mean we have to **finish up**?" he asked.

The kids all laughed.

"Okay, everyone, open your new books to page one hundred twelve," Mrs. Kelly said.

George smiled. Page 112 was the last page of the book. They were starting at the end. That was *very* backward!

Chapter 9

When George's class went to phys ed, Mr. Trainer was standing in the middle of the gym. Even *that* was backward in a way. Mr. Trainer was **hardly ever** in school. Usually, Mrs. Kelly substituted for him, which stunk because Mrs. Kelly made the kids do weird things, **like square-dance**.

"So what are we going to do today?" Mr. Trainer asked the kids.

Huh?

"Don't *you* know?" Sage asked. "You're the gym teacher."

"No, I'm not," Mr. Trainer told her.

Double huh?

"Today is Backward Day," Mr. Trainer reminded them. "Which means **I'm a kid**. One of you will be the gym teacher."

George laughed. Mr. Trainer was here, but they were *still* having a substitute!

"Ooooh, me, me!" Louie shouted out before anyone else could.

"Yeah, him, him!" Max and Mike exclaimed at once.

"Okay, Louie, the class is all yours," Mr. Trainer said. "What game is your class going to play?"

"I'm in charge," Louie said. "And that means we'll play . . ."

The kids all knew what he was going to say . . .

"Killer ball!" they shouted.

"Exactly," Louie said as he grabbed a big, red ball.

George was not a fan of killer ball. It was a game Louie had made up. It was sort of like dodgeball, only meaner. **Louie always aimed for George.**

Louie took the whistle that Mr. Trainer wore on a chain around his neck and put it on. He **blasted the whistle**, and the game began.

Bam! Mike slammed the ball at George as hard as he could. **Somehow George managed to duck just in time.** The ball hit the wall, and Julianna grabbed it. The ball whizzed across the gym and blasted Max.

"Ouch!" Max shouted. He frowned. It was never cool to be the first person whacked in killer ball.

Next, the ball came flying at Mr. Trainer. He caught it with no trouble.

"Nice catch," Julianna shouted.

"Now what do I do?" Mr. Trainer asked Louie.

"Throw it, and try to slam someone," Louie said.

Mr. Trainer threw the ball. *Bam!*
Alex was out.

George scooped up the ball and got
ready to throw. But before he could,
George felt something weird inside.
Bubbles! *Lots* of them. Bouncing around
deep down in his belly.

Oh no! The super burp was back!
And it wanted out. This was *ba-a-ad*.

Really *ba-a-ad*!

Ping-pong! Bing-bong! The bubbles were **bouncing all around**. George shut his mouth tight so the burp couldn't slip out of his mouth.

But the burp was smart—it turned around and started bouncing down the other way. *Uh-oh!*

Was his worst fear about to come true? **A *backward* burp?** No way was

George going to let that happen! He started bouncing up and down. Then he stood on his hands. He was trying to confuse the burp. This way, the bubbles wouldn't know which way was up and which way was down.

The kids laughed. All except Alex. **He knew what was going on.**

Louie looked mad. He blew on the whistle. "There's no pogo-ing in killer ball!" he shouted. "You gotta throw."

But George kept jumping up and down. Harder and harder he jumped. The bubbles in his belly went up and down and up and down. And then . . .

Whoosh! Suddenly, George felt something go pop in the bottom of his belly. All the air rushed right out of him. **The super burp was gone.**

George threw his hands up in the air. Then he sent the ball flying across the room!

"Ouch!" Louie shouted as the ball **slammed him right in the belly**!

Uh-oh. The kids all stopped moving. No one said a word.

"Okay, game over," Louie shouted suddenly.

"Why?" Julianna asked.

"I'm the teacher," Louie told her. "I don't have to give a reason."

George rolled his eyes. **Talk about a sore loser.**

But George was no loser. He was a *winner*—big time. After all, he had just won the battle of **the backward belch**.

And that was a huge Y-R-O-T-C-I-V. Victory . . . backward style.

Chapter 10

The next day during morning announcements, WEBS TV ran Julianna's taped interview with George. George felt kind of **like a celebrity** as he sat with his classmates and watched himself on TV.

"So, when did you discover you had a **talent for spelling**?" Julianna asked George.

George shrugged. "I guess second grade. That's when we started having spelling tests in one of my old schools."

"How many schools have you gone to?"

"Mmmm, let's see. This is the fourth. My dad is in the army, so my family has moved a lot."

"Does a talent for spelling run in your family?" Julianna asked him. "Are your mom and dad spelling champs, too?"

"He's not **the champ yet**," Louie called out. "He hasn't even *been* to the county-wide spelling bee."

"Well, **he's the champ here**," Sage reminded Louie.

The kids focused their attention back on the TV. Julianna was asking George another  question. "What's **the toughest word** you can spell?" Julianna asked on the tape.

"There's this one HUGE word," George answered. "My grandma taught it to me on the phone last night. It's *antidisestablishmentarianism*."

Louie rolled his eyes. "I can't believe you're all watching George spell on TV," he said.

"I believe it," Max said.

"Me too," Mike added. "Because that's what we're doing. Can't you see the TV, Louie? Do you want me to move so you can get **a better view**?"

"No," Louie grumbled. "I can see just fine."

George **smiled** as he watched himself standing on his head on TV and spelling upside down. Louie was j-e-a-l-o-u-s. And that was just f-i-n-e with George!

On the Saturday morning of the spelling bee, George put on his new shirt and slacks. Then he went downstairs.

"Ten-hut!" George's dad shouted as George walked into the living room.

George stood at attention while his mom inspected him.

She looked down to make sure his shoes were tied. She looked up to make sure his bow tie was straight.

"These new underpants are too tight," George complained. "And these suspenders are yanking my pants up too high. Can't I just wear jeans?" He tilted his head and gave his mom **a huge smile**. That was his special face. His mom always gave in when he gave **her the special face**.

But not today. His mom wasn't budging. "The underpants are tight because they're new. They'll loosen up. And the suspenders are important. They'll make sure your pants don't start to slide down during the spelling bee." She licked her fingers.

"Oh no, Mom!" George begged. "**Not the spit.** Please."

Yes, the spit. George's mom rubbed her spitty fingers **all over his hair** to make it lay flat. *Yuck!*

Finally, George's mom decided he

was good to go. "Let's get in the car!" she announced.

"I smell success!" George's dad said.

"Success. S-u-c-c-e-s-s," George spelled. He sure hoped his dad was right!

During the car ride, George's stomach felt funny.

"Are you okay, George?" his dad asked, glancing in the rearview mirror.

Was his dad kidding? George was on his way to the county-wide spelling bee and was plenty nervous. Besides that,

his tighty whities were practically strangling his rear. He had his mom's spit in his hair. And now he felt like he was going to **throw up**. How was a guy supposed to be okay through all of that?

Especially a guy who was worried about **a certain massive, magical megaburp** that always popped up at **exactly the wrong time**. And a county-wide spelling bee was just about the wrongest time there was.

George was definitely NOT okay.

"It's okay to feel a little nervous, honey," his mom said. "Spell *nervous* for me."

"N-E-R-V-O-U-S."

"I told you, I smell success," his dad told him.

George smiled a little. He sure hoped so.

Chapter 11

By the time George stepped out of the car in front of the community center, it felt as if his tighty whities were coming alive. They were so tight, he **practically had a wedgie**. George tried to reach in and pull them down. But then *he saw Louie.* He was standing right next to the refreshment stand in the lobby.

"What are you doing here?" George asked him nervously.

"My whole family is here," Louie answered. "We come every year, since Sam was in the bee. You know, when he got his ribbon."

Bummer. It was bad enough that George was wearing weird clothes and being attacked by his underwear. Now Louie was going to be sitting there in the audience staring at him and just waiting for him **to mess up**.

Luckily, Alex, Chris, and Julianna were coming, too. A moment later, they all walked in the door. Mrs. Kelly had brought them to cheer George on. Chris was carrying a big sign. He had drawn a picture of a kid that looked like George wearing **a superhero costume** on it. The picture said: George Brown, Super Speller!

"That's really cool," George told Chris. **"Thanks."**

"Hey, champ, how are you feeling?" Julianna asked. She rolled her hands into fists and pretended to pound at George like a boxer. "Are you ready to get out there and **show them what you're made of**?"

"I guess," George said. Right now it felt like **tiny ants** were running up and down his body. He felt all tingly and itchy. Nerves could do that to a guy.

"We're very proud, George," Mrs. Kelly said.

"I just hope I don't mess up in front of everybody." He gave Alex a look. "I don't want to **look like a jerk**."

Alex nodded. He knew exactly what George was talking about. "Just don't think about it," he whispered to his best friend. "Be positive."

"P-o-s-i-t-i-v-e," George spelled. He was trying to be.

"This place is really filling up," Julianna said.

"Will all the contestants please come to the stage," the moderator announced suddenly.

"That's your cue," Julianna said.

"Good luck, son," his father said. He gave George **a salute**.

"Straighten your bow tie," his mother added.

George saluted his dad. He straightened his tie. Then he walked up the steps to the stage and sat down on one of the metal chairs. It wasn't very comfortable. It was hard and cold.

Metal. M-e-t-a-l, George spelled. He smiled a little. Okay, he could handle this. After all, he was **a good speller**. And he'd been practicing a lot. It was going to be okay.

"Okay, let's have our spellers introduce themselves," the moderator said.

A small girl with long, red hair walked up to the microphone. "My name is S-a-r-a *without* an *h*," she said. "Sara Lemmon from Pumpersnickety Elementary School."

Next, a short boy with curly hair walked up to the mic. "I'm Carlton Smith from Bandago Bay Elementary School."

Now it was George's turn. He walked up to the microphone and said, "My name is George—"

But before he could say his whole name, George felt something **brewing in the pit of his stomach**. Something bingy and bongy. Something that pinged and ponged.

Oh no! This was what George had been afraid of! **This was his worst n-i-g-h-t-m-a-r-e!**

The super burp was back!

George clapped his hand over his mouth.

But this burp was strong. Already it had **bing-bonged** over George's bladder and **ping-ponged** its way past his pancreas. That burp wanted out—**bad**. And his tighty whities were actually **squeezing** it right out of him!

Darn tighty whities! From now on, George was wearing nothing but boxers. But that wasn't gonna help right now! George's eyes nearly **bugged out** of his head. And that's when he spotted Louie. He was looking right at George . . .

and laughing.

"See, I told you guys he was gonna freak out!" George heard Louie tell the other kids.

George had to get out of there. He couldn't let Louie be right. He couldn't freak out **in front of the whole auditorium**.

George leaped off the stage and ran for the door.

"George, where are you going?" the moderator asked.

But George didn't answer. He couldn't. He was afraid if he opened his mouth the burp would burst right out of him.

Ping-pong. Bing-bong!

George kept going, although his extra-tighty tighty whities made running hard. He threw the door of the community center open and raced outside. And then . . .

A giant burp ripped right out of him. It was loud. It was strong. It was magic. And it was *ba-a-ad*!

Chapter 12

Alex, Julianna, and Chris came rushing outside to find George. Mrs. Kelly hurried out right after them.

"George, we understand you're nervous, but get back inside," Mrs. Kelly said. "The spelling bee is starting **any minute**."

Just then, George's eyes spotted a bed of red and yellow flowers in a garden near the playground. His feet started running toward them.

"Dude! No!" Alex shouted. "Don't go over there."

"What's he doing?" Chris asked.

Now Louie was standing with the other kids and Mrs. Kelly. "He's freaking out," Louie told Chris. **"Just like always."**

George jumped into the bed of flowers and began dancing around on his tiptoes like **a crazed ballerina**. He yanked a flower out of the ground and stuck it behind his ear.

"Earwax," he said. "E-a-r-w-a-x."

"George, get out of there!"

George's ears recognized his father's voice. **He sounded mad.**

George wanted to get away from the flowers. He really did. **But he couldn't.** No matter how hard he tried.

Instead, he picked another flower and put it up to his nose to take a sniff.

"Achoo!" George's nose sneezed. Green, slimy boogers flew out of his nose.

"Booger," he said. "B-o-o-g-e-r."

George's arms reached up into the air as he danced. George's nose took a sniff at his pits. *Pee-yew!* They did not smell flowery.

"Stinky," he said. "S-t-i-n-k-y."

"You're getting your new pants all dirty."

That was George's mother. She sounded even madder than his dad.

Just then, George heard something else.

Bzzzzzzzz. It was a bee. And not a *spelling* bee, either. This was the kind of bee that—STUNG!

The bee's stinger went **right into George's rear end**.

Whoosh! At just that moment George felt something pop deep in the bottom of his belly. All the wind rushed out of him.

The super burp was gone. **Wow! Did his rear hurt!**

George opened his mouth to shout, "Ouch!" And that was exactly what came out.

A few minutes later, George was up on the stage with the other contestants. His rear end was very sore. But so what? He was still **one lean, mean spelling machine**. And he wasn't burping.

"Okay, let's start this spelling bee," the moderator said. "We'll begin with George Brown from Edith B. Sugarman Elementary School. George, your word is *skeleton*."

Oh good, George thought. *An easy one.* "Skeleton," he said. "S-k-e-l-e-t-o-n."

"Correct," the moderator said.

George smiled.

"Our next word is for Howard Harriman from Dwingledorf Elementary," the moderator said. "Howard, your word is *homonym.*"

Howard looked nervous. "Homonym. H-o-m-o-n-i-m," he spelled.

"I'm sorry," the moderator said. "That is incorrect."

George tried hard not to smile. That would be acting like a bad sport. And if there was anything the new, improved George was, it was a good s-p-o-r-t.

By the end of the fifth round, it was down to three spellers: George, Carlton, and a short girl with long, black hair named Mei Lee.

"Okay, George," the moderator said. "Spell *camera.*"

"Camera," George repeated. "C-a-m-e-r-a. Camera."

"Correct," the moderator told him.

Alex, Julianna, and Chris all cheered. Louie just sat there and **glared** at George. It was like he *wanted* him to lose.

"Mei, your word is *whistle,*" the moderator said.

Mei Lee took a deep breath. "W-h-i-s-l-e," she spelled. "Whistle."

Uh-oh. Mei Lee had **forgotten the silent *t* in whistle**. You had to be careful with that one.

"I'm sorry," the moderator said. "That is incorrect."

Mei Lee looked like she was going to cry as she walked off the stage.

"Carlton, it's your turn," the moderator told the curly-haired boy standing next

to George. "Can you spell *whistle* correctly?"

Carlton gulped. **Big beads of sweat formed on his forehead.** This could be it. Carlton was folding under the pressure.

"Whistle. W-h-i-s-t-l-e," Carlton spelled. His voice cracked a little. "Whistle."

George frowned. Darn it. This Carlton kid was really good.

"Correct," the moderator said. She turned to George. "Your word is *vaporize.*"

Uh-oh. That wasn't a word George had studied. He closed his eyes and tried to picture the word. But it was **hard to concentrate.** His

rear end still hurt. And even through his closed eyes, George could feel Louie **glaring at him**, wishing he would lose. But he could also feel his friends and parents staring at him, wishing he would win.

"Vaporize," George said slowly. "V-a-p-u-r-i-z-e. Vaporize."

The moderator took a deep breath. "I'm sorry," she said. "That is incorrect."

There was a gasp in the crowd.

Now George knew how Mei Lee felt. **It stunk to get this close and still lose.** Of course he hadn't lost yet. Carlton could still spell the word wrong, and then there would be another round.

"Carlton, can you spell *vaporize*?" the moderator asked.

Carlton took a deep breath.

"Vaporize," he repeated. "V-a-p-o-r-i-z-e. Vaporize."

"Correct," the moderator said. **"That means Carlton is our winner!"**

Chapter 13

"That's a cool trophy," Alex told George a few minutes later when everyone was standing in the lobby of the community center.

George's **second-place trophy** wasn't as big as the one Carlton was carrying around, but it was still pretty nice.

Julianna held up her video camera. "I want to show some footage on Monday's sportscast," she explained. **"Nobody from Sugarman has ever come in second before."**

"I'm proud of you, son," his father told him. "You did a great job."

His mom gave him **a squeeze**. "Me too," she said.

"I'm sorry about . . . before," George told his parents and friends.

"It's okay," his mom said. "We all do weird things when we're nervous."

"Yeah, that's what it was," Alex said. "Nerves."

George smiled. Good old Alex. He was always there to cover for him.

Just then, Mrs. Kelly began dancing around in a circle. She raised her hands high. She moved her hands low. She spun around. She was doing a cheer. "Congratulations, George Brown, on **your glorious victory**! Congratulations, George Brown. You're a great speller, we all can see."

George laughed. Mrs. Kelly was

definitely weird. W-e-i-r-d. Just then, George caught a glimpse of Louie. He was with his family, mouthing something at him. George tried to read his lips.

"Loser," Louie mouthed. **"Loser."**

George pretended he couldn't figure out what Louie was trying to tell him.

Just then, Louie's brother, Sam, started walking over to George. He shook George's hand. "Great job," he said. "You spelled a whole lot of hard words." Sam looked over at his brother. **"Right, Louie?"**

"Uh . . . yeah . . . ," Louie told his brother. "I was just gonna say that."

Just then, George felt something weird brewing in his body. He shut his mouth tight. There was no way he was letting any burp make him go **all crazy** again!

"Are you okay?" Sam asked George.

George nodded. He tried to keep his lips shut tight. But suddenly . . .

Hiccup. A hiccup slipped from his lips. George just stood there.

"*Hiccup,*" he said again. Louie started laughing at him. But George didn't care. Let Louie laugh. Anyone could get hiccups. **They were nice and normal.** And *harmless.*

Not like super burps. George rubbed his tush. The bee sting still hurt. Super burps were **a major pain in the you-know-where**!

About the Author

Nancy Krulik is the author of more than 150 books for children and young adults including three *New York Times* best sellers and the popular Katie Kazoo, Switcheroo books. She lives in New York City with her family, and many of George Brown's escapades are based on things her own kids have done. (No one delivers a good burp quite like Nancy's son, Ian!) Nancy's favorite thing to do is laugh, which comes in pretty handy when you're trying to write funny books!

About the Illustrator

Aaron Blecha was raised by a school of giant squid in Wisconsin and now lives with his family by the English seaside. He works as an artist designing toys, animating cartoons, and illustrating books, including the Zombiekins and The Rotten Adventures of Zachary Ruthless series. You can enjoy more of his weird creations at www.monstersquid.com.